Magic Rescue Vets

Snowball the Baby Yeti

Melody Lockhart

Titles in this series

1. Oona the Unicorn
2. Jade the Gem Dragon
3. Blaze the Phoenix
4. Holly the Flying Horse
5. Snowball the Baby Yeti
6. Suki the Sea Dragon

This edition published in 2022 by Arcturus Publishing Limited
26/27 Bickels Yard, 151–153 Bermondsey Street,
London SE1 3HA

Author: Melody Lockhart
Story editor: Xanna Eve Chown
Illustrator: Morgan Huff
Designer: Jeni Child
Managing editor: Joe Harris

CH010410NT
Supplier 10, Date 0722, PI 00002077

Printed in the UK

MIX
Paper from
responsible sources
FSC® C018072
www.fsc.org

Contents

Starfall Forest Map

WEATHER-OR-NOT CAVES

OH-NO VOLCANOES

COZY CAMPSITE

FAIRGROUND FIELDS

ELFINGTON CASTLE

KELP TOWN

SOFT HENGE

COTTON-TOP MOUNTAINS

LOOKING-GLASS LAKE

CALICO COMFREYS

RAINBOW RIVER

MAZE WOOD

GNOME TOWN

TILTING TOWER

RAINBOW COASTER HILLS

WILLOW COTTAGE

MOONFLOWER MEADOWS

SPRINGHAVEN

TOPSY-TURVY TREES

Chapter 1
Bugbears and Bubbles

"**W**ell, the bugbears are clean, but the room is an absolute mess!" Rosie laughed as she wiped soapsuds from her hair.

Everywhere she looked, there were soapy bubbles and puddles of water. The bathtub, on the other hand, was nearly empty. Rosie's best friend, Kat, was busy trying to dry three small, wet bears with spotty red-and-black fur as the creatures rolled around happily.

At that moment, a bespectacled woman in a white coat appeared in the doorway. "Are you bathing the bugbears, kiddos," she asked, "or are you having a waterfight?"

"I think it might be a bit of both!" said Kat. "Would you like to join in, Doctor Clarice?"

Kat and Rosie loved helping out at Calico Comfrey's Veterinary Surgery in the heart of Starfall Forest. It was certainly no ordinary vet's! The forest was a safe haven for magical creatures—from graceful unicorns to singing starfish—and Doctor Clarice was one of the vets who cared for them all. Rosie's house, Willow Cottage, was right next to Starfall, so it was easy to visit the surgery whenever the girls liked.

Kat picked up a glass jar full of the sparkling creatures they'd washed off the bugbears. "Natternits are cute," she said. "It's a shame they made the poor bears itch!"

"They really should have known not to play near a natternit nest," said Doctor Clarice. "But the truth is I'm actually pleased that the place is such a mess."

"Really? Why's that?" Rosie asked.

"It gives me a chance to try out my latest invention!" the vet replied, pushing her glasses up her nose. "I call it the de-messifier."

Doctor Clarice was not just a vet—she was also an inventor. Rosie watched as she produced a wand with a shiny, silver ball at the end from inside her coat. At the press of a button, the ball started to spin.

At once, all the soapy bubbles in the room began to bunch together until they made one big, pink pile in the bathtub.

"Not bad!" said Doctor Clarice. "Doctor Hart will be pleased—she hates cleaning!"

"Where *is* Doctor Hart?" Kat asked.

"She's off in the forest collecting plant samples with Doctor Morel. I'm going to

join them after we take the natternits home.
Would you girls like a lift home on the way?"

"Yes please!" chorused Kat and Rosie.

No matter how many times Rosie rode on
the vets' flying carpet, it was always exciting.
She loved the way the wind felt as it rushed
through her hair and the pretty bubbles that
streamed out as it sped through the sky. All
too soon, they arrived at Willow Cottage.

"I remember the first time I saw the carpet,"
Rosie said dreamily, as she and Kat climbed
down. "I was looking out of my window just
after we'd moved here."

To her surprise, Doctor Clarice looked
alarmed. "Oh dear," said the vet. "I'll have to
be more careful. Starfall's magic is meant to
be a secret. We don't want another disaster!"

"What do you mean?" asked Rosie. But the
flying carpet had already whooshed away.

Kat and Rosie hugged goodbye, and Kat set off down the road for her own home. Rosie went into the kitchen where her parents were busy cooking dinner.

"Hi, pumpkin," said her dad. "Have you and Kat been doing something fun?"

"Yes," said Rosie. "We gave some bugbears a bath."

Her mother smiled. "Let me guess," she said. "Bugbears are ... tiny beetles with a loud roar?"

"No, Mama," laughed Rosie. "They're bears with spotty fur and antennae."

"Of course!" her dad said with a wink.

Rosie shrugged. It was obvious that her parents didn't believe her. She decided to go up to her room and pack her schoolbag for the next day.

She'd just reached the stairs when

she heard her father sigh.

"It's great that she's got such a vivid imagination," he said to her mother, "but I sometimes wish I knew what she was really doing, instead of hearing all these funny stories. She used to tell me everything ..."

"I've got an idea," said Mama. "I'm going to Opal City for a conference tomorrow. I won't be back till Sunday morning. Why don't you take Rosie and Kat camping while I'm away? Make some memories!"

Rosie rushed back down the stairs. "Camping?" she said excitedly. "Yes please!"

Mama laughed. "Hold on," she said. "Dad hasn't agreed yet."

But Dad was as excited as Rosie. In fact, he was already rummaging in a drawer looking for his map. "If I remember correctly, there's a campsite right on the edge of the forest," he said. Dad had lived in Springhaven when he a boy, before his family moved to Opal City. He spread out the map on the kitchen table and pointed to a yellow blob in the corner. "There," he said triumphantly. "Cozy Campsite. Near the Cotton-Top Mountains, look!"

Rosie looked at the map. Starfall Forest was shown as a big green shape, with the Rainbow River marked in blue running through it. There was no clue to

the magical places hidden within it—like
Grumpling Grove or the Lollipop Orchard.

"If I'm right, some rather unusual animals
live around there," said Dad.

Rosie stared at him in surprise. Surely
he wasn't talking about magical creatures?
"Exactly how ... unusual?" she asked.

"That's funny," said Dad, suddenly looking
puzzled. "I can't really remember."

Rosie phoned Kat right away. She was sure her friend would be as excited as she was! But when Kat answered the phone, it was hard to make out what she was saying. All Rosie could hear were the strange muffled thumps and shouts in the background.

"What's going on?" she shouted. "It sounds like you've invited a flappopotamus to tea!"

"It's Jordan and Jayden," sighed Kat. Her twin brothers were always up to some kind of noisy mischief. "They've covered

the stairs in blankets and pillows so they can toboggan down them!"

In between the bumps and thuds, Rosie explained about the camping trip. "Dad wants to leave after school tomorrow," she said. "So you'll need to bring your pajamas, sleeping bag, and snacks ... Lots of snacks!"

"I'll have to ask my parents," Kat said, happily. "But I know they'll say yes!" There was a sudden splash from behind her.

"Was that Jordan or Jayden?" Rosie asked.

"It's Brianna," sighed Kat. Brianna was her baby sister. "I think she's trying to wash the cat ... It's never quiet in this house!"

Rosie grinned. Kat's family had lots of pets—one iguana, two cats, four hamsters, and six chickens. Even though Kat sometimes complained, Rosie knew she wouldn't have it any other way.

Chapter 2
Desdemona Downspout

The next day at school, Miss Lavender had a surprise for Rosie's class. "A famous writer has come to visit us from Opal City," she said.

Rosie stared curiously at the woman standing next to her teacher. She had enormous glasses and wild hair and smelled strongly of ... was that garlic?

"Hello kiddiewinks," she said. "My name's Desdemona Downspout, but my fans call me Deedee. I write books about mysterious animals. Who here has heard of ... the yeti?"

All the children raised their hands.

"And who believes that yetis are real?" asked the writer.

Rosie saw that only a few hands were still raised. She had never met a yeti, but she had seen a lot stranger animals in Starfall Forest! She decided to keep her hand up.

"Here are the facts," said Desdemona. "We know that yetis are shy creatures who rarely let themselves be seen. However, in the last few weeks, several yetis have been spotted near Starfall Forest. One in New Town, another in Crumble Creek, and yet another—yes— in Springhaven! It can only mean one thing …" She paused dramatically. "Starfall Forest is crammed with yetis."

Desdemona began to hand out paper and pencils. "Now, I know what you're all thinking," she said. "Wouldn't it be wonderful if somebody wrote a bestselling book about these mysterious creatures?" She pointed out the window where the trees of Starfall could be seen over the schoolyard wall. "Well, I'm going to do it," she said. "But I need your help. I need you all to draw me any … unusual … creatures that you've spotted around here."

Rosie felt a little alarmed. She wasn't sure that Desdemona could be trusted. All the vets agreed that it was important to keep the magical creatures of Starfall Forest a secret in order to protect them. "What do we draw?" she hissed at Kat.

Kat didn't look at all worried. In fact, she was smiling. "I'll describe an animal for you,"

she said. "Start with a long, furry body …
then add two green eyes … and long, sharp
claws."

"It sounds a bit scary," said Rosie. "Does it
live in the forest?"

"Not really," said Kat starting to laugh.
"It's Buttons!"

Then, Rosie couldn't help laughing too.
Buttons the cat was one of Kat's pets.

"He's definitely unusual," Kat added. "Last
night, he fell asleep in the dishwasher."

By the time the lesson was over, Rosie had drawn most of Kat's pets, including both her cats, Bertie and Buttons. She couldn't help wondering what the rest of the class had drawn, so she volunteered to stay behind and collect all of the pictures for Desdemona.

"Thank you, my darling," beamed Desdemona.

"I'm worried about the secret of the forest getting out," Rosie explained to Kat in a whisper. "Aren't you?"

Kat shook her head. "You know what happens when people try to go in," she said and followed the other children into the schoolyard. Rosie grinned. There was an enchantment on the forest that made people forget what they were doing and turn away when they tried to enter it.

As Rosie collected the pictures, she was

relieved to see that most of them showed foxes, mice, and squirrels. There was a dragon—but Rosie had met a real-life dragon, and she could tell that whoever had drawn this cross-eyed one had not!

The very last picture she picked up looked a lot like one of the stinky, green boombadgers that lived in the forest. Quickly, she scrunched up the paper and dropped it in the trash before anyone saw it.

Miss Lavender was talking to Desdemona over by the classroom window. Rosie noticed that she had her hands on her hips and was using her stern voice.

"I think you've confused the children," Rosie heard her teacher say. "It's one thing to ask them to draw a mythical creature—but it's quite another to ask them if they have actually seen one! You're confusing fiction and reality."

"No, no, no," insisted Desdemona. "Yetis are real—and they're living very close to this school. Look, I have a photograph." She took out a blurry photo and waved it in the teacher's face.

Miss Lavender frowned. "I'm afraid that is not very convincing," she said.

"Oh!" exclaimed Desdemona, throwing her hands up in the air. "You sound just like my publishers in Opal City. They're always saying, 'You need evidence, Deedee!' or 'This is your last chance, Deedee!' or 'We're not printing any more of your books without proof, Deedee!' Don't you see, Miss Lavender? If I don't find any yetis in Starfall Forest, my whole career is over!"

Rosie decided to leave them to it. She put the rest of the drawings on Miss Lavender's desk in a neat pile, then went to find Kat.

Kat and some of her friends were in the schoolyard inventing a game called Yeti Hide-And-Seek.

"We're all yetis," Kat explained, "and Luca is a famous writer. That bench is his base. He counts to ten while we hide."

Luca shut his eyes and started to count, and everyone scattered. Kat dragged Rosie across the yard, and they hid behind a wall.

"If he finds us, we have to roar like a yeti and chase him back to his base," said Kat.

"Do yetis roar?" giggled Rosie.

"I don't know," said Kat. "But we can look for one on our camping trip and find out!"

"No we can't," Rosie said with a sigh. "We'll be with Dad, and he won't be able to come into the forest with us because of the enchantment." She wished that her parents believed her when she told them about the magical animals. She'd love to show them Calico Comfrey's surgery. She knew they could be trusted with the secret, because they loved animals just as much as she did.

Kat gave her a hug. "We'll still have fun," she said comfortingly.

"Of course we will," said Rosie brightening up. "Sleeping under the stars ... singing songs around the campfire ... eating s'mores ... It will be amazing!"

Chapter 3
Cozy Campsite

After school, the girls walked home to Rosie's house, talking excitedly all the way. Kat had a backpack loaded with all the things she would need for the trip.

"Hi, girls!" called Dad. "I've nearly finished packing the car. Mama's already gone to her conference in Opal City, but she's left you something in the kitchen."

The girls dashed into the house and found two blueberry muffins with a note that read, "Have a great trip!"

It was a warm day, and spring flowers were blooming along the roadside as Dad

drove through Springhaven. On one side of the road, there were fields. On the other side, the trees of Starfall Forest stretched away into the distance. Clumps of pretty blue flowers were clustered about their roots.

Suddenly, a three-tailed creature—a magical kitsune—darted across the road.

"Was that a fox?" Dad asked, turning onto the bumpy track that led to Cozy Campsite. He parked the car, and everyone clambered out, glad to stretch their legs. "The Forest was full of wildlife when I was a boy."

The campsite was in a large field, surrounded by trees, with the Rainbow River bubbling gently along one side. It was strange to think that this was the same river that ran through the forest, Rosie thought. It was narrower here, more like a stream, and the bridge across it was small and wooden. In the forest, it gushed past at a great pace, and there were magical bridges made of shimmering rainbows.

The only other visitor at the site was in a shiny, silver motor home. Rosie nudged Kat. Someone was waving from one of its windows.

"It's Desdemona Downspout!" exclaimed Kat. "What is she doing here?"

"Looking for yetis, of course," groaned Rosie. Her earlier worries came flooding back. "Let's go and say hi."

Desdemona's van was covered in strange,

mystical patterns and had a peculiar satellite dish spinning around on the top. As they got nearer, the girls wrinkled up their noses at the strong smell of garlic.

"Hello, kiddiewinks!" called Desdemona. "Sorry about the smell. I've just mixed up some more Monster-Be-Gone. It's my own recipe. I wear it in this pouch round my neck to keep any nasty creatures away. You can't be too careful in my line of work!"

"What's in it?" Rosie asked.

"Lots of exotic herbs," Desdemona said airily. "Oh, and garlic to scare off vampires."

"Have you ever met a vampire?" Rosie asked curiously.

"No," admitted Desdemona. "But that means that my pouch is working!"

That sounded like one of Dad's terrible jokes, Rosie thought. But Desdemona looked very serious …

"Now, my darlings," Desdemona continued. "Would you like to see my yeti?"

Rosie felt an icy shiver run down her spine. Had the famous author actually found a yeti? How had she managed to enter the forest? What would the vets say? She relaxed when she saw that Desdemona was holding out a fluffy toy.

"Isn't it adorable?" Desdemona asked. "When I've finished writing, I'm going to have thousands made. One free with every book!"

"That's a ... nice idea," said Kat.

"Yetis live in caves high in the mountains," said Desdemona, "so you can guess where I'm starting my expedition tomorrow morning." She pointed at the snow-covered peaks of the Cotton-Top Mountains. "I hope they are easy to catch."

Rosie frowned. "You actually want to catch one?" she asked.

"Only on camera," said Desdemona with a laugh.

Inside the motor home, the walls were lined with crinkly foil. There were photos and old newspaper clippings pinned everywhere. Rosie was surprised to find that she recognized a lot of the places in the pictures. One showed a tree being cut down with a chainsaw in Grumpling Grove, while another was of a man in a strange, orange suit and mask standing in Lollipop

Orchard. He was holding some kind of box with thick, dark smoke belching out. What was he doing? Just the sight of it made Rosie want to cough! How scared the creatures must have been to see him.

"When were these pictures taken?" she asked.

"Twenty-five years ago," said Desdemona. "But there have been whispers about magical creatures living in Starfall Forest for hundreds of years." She peered closer at the girls. "In fact, Miss Lavender told me that you two often talk about unusual animals. Is that true?"

"Yes," said Rosie.

"No!" said Kat—at exactly the same time.

Desdemona looked confused.

"I mean, yes, we do sometimes," said Kat feebly. "But it's just a game we play."

The girls said goodbye and wandered down to the river where they took off their shoes and socks.

"I didn't like those pictures," Rosie said gloomily, as they dipped their feet in the cold water. "It looked like a disaster! I can't believe the vets have never told us about it."

Kat frowned. "I think they have!" she said slowly. "Yesterday, Doctor Clarice said she didn't want another disaster."

Rosie gasped. Kat was right! She was about to reply when she felt something nibbling at her toes. A shoal of pretty fish was darting around her feet, their shimmering scales flicking from gold to silver and back again as they swam.

"They're gold-and-silver fish," said Kat. "Doctor Morel told me about them. The gnomes like to keep them as pets!" As she

spoke, the pattern on their scales started to form tiny, shiny letters. H … E … L … L … O.

"They're saying hello," said Rosie in amazement. "Hi, little fish. You shouldn't have swum so far upstream. If Desdemona sees you, she'll put you in her book!"

As if they understood, all the fish turned with a flick of their fins and swam away, deeper into the forest.

"Maybe we should warn the vets about Desdemona after all," said Kat thoughtfully.

Chapter 4
Snowball

*W*hen the girls got back to the car, Dad had unpacked all the bags and laid out a little picnic.

"That looks great," said Rosie. "But, er, where's the tent?"

Dad looked a bit sheepish. "I can't seem to find the tentpoles," he said.

"Maybe a hodgepodge took them," Kat whispered. Hodgepodges looked like purple hedgehogs with tiny, curly horns. They loved lining their nests with things they'd found.

Rosie shook her head. "I think he's left them at home by mistake," she said.

Luckily, Dad had a tarpaulin and some rope in the back of the car. The girls helped him haul it out and watched him hang the rope between two sturdy trees. They worked together to drape the large, blue tarpaulin over the rope, then piled blankets underneath it. Kat unrolled the sleeping bags, while Rosie twined string of lights in the branches.

"Well done girls," said Dad. Then, he wrinkled up his nose. "What on earth is that awful smell?"

"Coo-ee!" trilled a voice. "Only me!" Desdemona was bounding toward them holding a large bag. She was wearing a furry hat and had a peculiar pair of goggles pushed up her forehead.

"Hello," said Dad. "Miss ... er ...?"

"Call me Deedee!" said Desdemona. "I've brought some of my special mixture to keep you all safe."

Dad stared at the strange-looking woman sprinkling herbs around them. When Rosie explained that she had been visiting the school because she was writing a book about yetis, he looked even more confused. Then, he started to grin. "You know, scientists think we'll find Bigfoot one day," he said.

It was Desdemona's turn to look surprised. "Really?" she said.

"Yes," said Dad. "But not yet-i. Get it? Not yeti?"

Rosie pulled a face. "He's joking," she giggled. "Stop it, Dad!"

After Desdemona had gone back to her van, the girls went into the forest to collect wood for a campfire. It was starting to get dark, but the forest was peaceful and still. Lampbugs lit up the trees and the spiders were weaving sleepy patterns into their webs.

Rosie had soon collected an armful of sticks. She was about to suggest turning back when she heard a deep, thrumming noise that made the back of her neck tingle. She had never heard anything like it before. It didn't sound like an animal, or a person, or a machine ... but it seemed to be coming from a clearing ahead.

She could see that Kat had heard it too. Without saying a word, they moved toward the strange sound and found themselves in a clearing. A circle of large white shapes stood in the middle, humming and glowing gently in the moonlight.

Looking closer, Rosie could see that the shapes were columns and archways made up of fluffy pillows and blankets. For a moment, she just stood and stared. There was a mysterious feel to the place that prickled along her arms and legs. It felt like an ancient, powerful kind of magic.

Suddenly, there was a loud "HOOOOOP!" from overhead. Rosie gave a shriek of surprise, stumbling backward and clutching hold of Kat's arm.

"It's just a hoop owl," said Kat, laughing, but Rosie could see that she'd had a fright too. "Let's go back. Your dad will be wondering where we are."

Dad was very pleased with all the wood they'd found. He soon had a fire crackling away and helped the girls put together delicious, gooey s'mores to toast in the flames.

"Time for a campfire sing-along," said Dad, getting out his guitar.

"No old-timey rock though," laughed Rosie. "You promised."

"Don't worry," said Dad. "I can still remember the songs I learned when I was in the Springhaven Scouts. Do either of you two know 'Grufflegoat Grumble'?"

Rosie frowned. Grufflegoats lived in the Forest and had magical wool that changed shade with their mood. "What's a grufflegoat, Dad?" she asked—even though she knew the answer.

"No idea," said Dad cheerfully, starting

to strum the chords. It was a catchy tune, and soon both girls were joining in the chorus—"So now you know what to do if your grufflegoat is blue!"

After the sing-along, everyone got ready for bed and snuggled into their sleeping bags.

Rosie was just drifting off to slee when a loud growling filled the air.

"What's that?" squealed Kat.

But it was only Dad snoring. He was fast asleep, tired out after his busy day.

Rosie woke with a start to find Kat gently prodding her in the ribs. It was just before dawn and the sky was still dark. Dad was happily snoring away in his sleeping bag.

"What is it?" said Rosie woozily.

Kat put a finger to her lips to tell Rosie to be quiet. "I can hear something moving," she whispered. "I think there's an animal outside."

Rosie sat up and rubbed her eyes. She could hear it too—a snuffling, rustling noise.

Quietly, she crawled out of her sleeping bag and peered out into the moonlit field. Two blue eyes blinked back at her. It was a baby yeti!

The little creature looked a bit like a fuzzy white ball with large, furry feet. He had taken the lid off their cooler and turned it upside down, scattering cans and bottles all over the grass. In one hand, he held a cold, gooey s'more that must have been dropped during last night's feast. Keeping his twinkling eyes on Rosie, he stuffed it into his mouth and started to chew as quickly as possible.

"I think he's hungry," Rosie said.

"Or greedy," giggled Kat. "It looks like he's already eaten a whole package of hot dog buns."

Chapter 5
How to Hide a Yeti

"**R**emember what Desdemona said," Rosie said. "Yetis are very shy." She crawled slowly towards the creature, being careful not to make any sudden movements ... But to her surprise, the yeti gave a happy squeak, holding out his little arms and tottering forward to be picked up.

"Oh!" she said in surprise, as the little animal threw its arms around her in a hug. "I guess Desdemona was wrong."

Kat picked up an apple that had fallen out of the cooler, and held it out. With an excited snort, the yeti bounded over

and took it from her hand. Then, he snuggled into Rosie's lap and started to munch.

"He's adorable," said Kat, coming over to stroke his soft fur. "What shall we call him? He looks a bit like a furry snowball."

"Snowball suits him perfectly," Rosie said. "He's only a baby. I wonder where his parents are. Do you think he's lost?"

Rosie looked up at the snowy peaks of the Cotton-Top Mountains that rose high above the trees on the other side of the river. "Is that your home?" she asked.

The yeti nodded his head.

When Snowball had finished his apple, he wriggled off Rosie's lap to look around for more food. He found Kat's backpack and started to investigate. He snuffled into all the pockets and came out with a tube of toothpaste.

"Hey! Put that back," laughed Rosie as Snowball gave the tube a curious sniff, then popped it open. "Wait, Snowball. That's not food!"

Too late! Snowball had squeezed a huge

blob of sticky, minty toothpaste into his mouth. A strange expression came over his face. His eyes crossed, his nose began to twitch, and he gave a strange little cough.

"Oh no!" cried Kat, looking around for a bottle of water. "Quick, drink some of this," she said.

Snowball took a big gulp of water, but it only made things worse! Tiny white bubbles fizzed on his tongue, and his mouth filled up with minty froth. CRASH! He staggered backward into a stack of pots and pans, sending them flying.

"He'll wake Dad," said Rosie nervously. She glanced over her shoulder, but Dad snored on, unaware of the commotion taking place outside.

"It's worse than that," said Kat. "He's woken up Desdemona!"

Desdemona Downspout stood at the door of her motor home, rubbing her eyes. She peered out across the camp site.

"Quick, hide!" hissed Rosie, giving Snowball a little shove. The yeti looked at the girls' worried faces and scrambled to his feet, disappearing quickly behind the tent. Just in time! Desdemona was hurrying across the field toward them.

"Only me," called the writer. She raised her eyebrows at the sight of the

toothpaste-covered pots and pans. "What's going on over here?"

"Nothing," said Kat in an innocent voice. "We were just ... cleaning our teeth."

But Desdemona wasn't listening. "It looks like you've had a visitor in the night," she said. She had spotted something on the grass—minty white footprints that led around the side of the tent and into the bushes. She crouched down and started to follow the toothpaste trail.

"Oh, I don't think so," stammered Kat.

"I'm sure of it," said Desdemona.

Rosie held her breath as Desdemona disappeared behind the tent—then gave a huge sigh of relief when she appeared on the other side empty handed. Snowball must have hidden somewhere else.

"There's nothing here," sighed the writer.

Rosie saw Kat's eyes flick up to a nearby tree. Snowball was sitting on one of the lower branches with a michievous smile on his face. Oh no, Rosie thought. Any second now, Desdemona is going to look up and see him …

Kat must have had the same idea because she gave a loud shout and pointed to the far side of the campsite. "Look over there," she squeaked, grabbing the arm of Desdemona's dressing gown.

"What is it, my darling?" asked Desdemona. "What have you seen?"

"Something is hiding in that field," said Kat. "I think it might be a yeti!"

"Oh my," said Desdemona, her eyes lighting up. "Show me where."

As Kat dragged Desdemona away from the tent, Rosie turned her attention to Snowball.

She tried to help him down from the branch, but he giggled and shook his head. He liked it in the tree! Rosie sighed and hunted around for another apple. It seemed that food was the only way to make the yeti move. Sure enough, Snowball scrambled down the tree as soon as he saw the shiny, red apple and sat happily in Rosie's arms crunching away, as she searched for a better hiding place.

Rosie crept under the tarpaulin and stepped over her snoring Dad. Quickly and quietly, she grabbed her sleeping bag and bundled the little yeti inside. "Sorry, Snowball," she said, gently tossing two more apples in after him. He squeaked happily at the sight of more food and didn't seem to mind at all.

Then, she heard voices from outside ... Desdemona and Kat were back.

"I don't know how you can mistake a rabbit for a yeti," Desdemona said huffily. "For one thing, they are a completely different size."

Rosie tried not to laugh. She was about to leave the tent when Dad rolled over and gave a loud yawn. He was waking up! Rosie glanced at her wriggling sleeping bag. Dad was bound to notice the crunching noises coming from inside it and wonder what was going on.

"Only me," said Desdemona, suddenly poking her head under the tarpaulin. "Whatever have you go there?"

Rosie stared at the author in alarm. Her mind was a complete blank ...

Luckily, Kat came to her rescue. "I bet it's one of my little brothers!" she said, quickly. "They love playing hide and seek."

As Desdemona stomped back to her motor home, both girls let out a sigh of relief.

"We've got to get Snowball away," said Kat.

Rosie gave the sleeping bag a little shake, and Snowball crawled out. He snuffled in delight when she plopped Dad's baseball cap on his head. "It's a disguise," she whispered, then called to Dad that they were going to collect firewood.

"Mrrumph!" mumbled Dad. He always took ages to wake up in the mornings.

The girls grabbed a flashlight and wrapped Snowball in a blanket. They carried him into the forest, keeping well clear of Desdemona's van. They soon found themselves in the part of the forest they had been in the night before. The soft, white archways and columns were silent and still in the sunlight, but the air around

them seemed to twitch with magic. Snowball gave an excited wriggle and leaped out of Kat's arms, disappearing among the pillows.

"Come back!" said Rosie. Where had he gone? Calling his name, she started to walk around the circle—there was something about the strange, white shapes that made her want to keep to the outside. But the little yeti had completely vanished.

Rosie and Kat made their way back to the campsite, picking up more firewood on the way. Dad had tidied up the pots and pans and was opening a package of hot dogs.

"What would you like with them?" he asked. "I thought I'd brought some buns, but I can't find them anywhere."

Rosie knew exactly where they were—inside Snowball's belly! "Let's just eat them on their own," she said quickly. "Then we can have the leftover marshmallows for dessert."

"Do people usually eat dessert with breakfast?" Dad asked with a grin. "Okay, why not! We are on vacation, after all."

Rosie thought hot dogs and marshmallows were a great combination. Dad wasn't quite so sure. After breakfast, they took the empty plates to a wooden hut that stood in a corner of the campsite. Inside, there was a washroom with a shower, and outside there was a sink for washing cups and plates. As they rinsed the plates, the girls heard a very odd, warbling noise coming from inside the hut. Desdemona was singing in the shower!

"I bet her singing has scared off more vampires than that stinky necklace she wears," giggled Kat.

Chapter 6
The Camera Trap

Dad and the girls were playing a game of catch with a flying spinner, when Desdemona came rushing past them with a fluffy pink towel wrapped around her head. She was clutching her phone to her ear, and she waved at the girls excitedly.

"There's been another sighting," she called, climbing into her motor home and starting the engine. "A baby yeti in a baseball cap at Crumble Creek."

"Snowball?" Rosie whispered to Kat.

"It can't be," said Kat. "Crumble Creek is all the way on the other side of Starfall Forest.

It would take
a whole day
to get there."

Rosie frowned.
"We don't know
much about yetis,"
she said. "Perhaps they're
really fast runners."

"Hey," called Dad. "Did you hear about the man and the yeti who had a race? The yeti won it ... by a *big foot!*"

Rosie couldn't help smiling. "Your jokes are terrible, Dad," she said.

"Yet he still makes them," said Kat. "Get it? YETI still makes them!"

Everyone laughed. Dad put down the flying spinner and looked at the trees that lined the edges of the campsite. "Who wants to go on a nice, long walk in Starfall Forest?" he asked.

Kat and Rosie followed Dad toward the forest, wondering what would happen when the enchantment started working.

"Have you ever wondered why the forest never turns us away?" Kat whispered.

Rosie shrugged. "Doctor Hart thinks it's something to do with Willow Cottage."

As they reached the trees, Dad stopped and scratched his head. "Now, what am I doing?" he said. He took off his backpack and sat down beside a patch of pretty blue flowers. "Wasn't I was planning to tidy up the tent?"

There was a buzzing sound from Rosie's pocket. Her magical crystalzoometer was starting to spin. She glanced at Kat and saw that her friend's machine was buzzing too. The vets had given the magical devices to the girls to let them know when there was an animal in trouble nearby.

"Shall we go on without you, Dad?" Rosie asked. "We'll be back for lunch."

"Good idea," said Dad, sounding relieved.

Rosie was sad to leave him behind, but there was no time to think about that now. They had to find the injured animal—whatever it might be. She grabbed Kat's hand and they followed the spinning arrow through the bushes and past a tree full of baby grumplings who waved happily as they passed.

The girls came to a place where the Rainbow River split in two and crossed both parts using a rickety rope bridge. On the other side, there was a rocky path that sloped upward, and Rosie realized that they were in the foothills of the Cotton-Top Mountains.

"We need to go up," said Kat, looking at her crystalzoometer.

The winding track that led up the mountain wasn't too steep, and the girls admired the beautiful spring flowers that lined the way.

"I don't think I've ever seen a flower quite like that before," said Rosie, pointing to a spotty purple tulip. Its delicate leaves shivered as they walked past, and then—to the girls' surprise—it gave a loud sneeze.

"Maybe it's an atchoo-lip!" Kat joked.

That made Rosie laugh. She looked around to see if there were any more funny flowers—

and spotted something even stranger. Sitting on the ground, just a short distance ahead, was a plate of cupcakes covered in pink frosting. The girls went to take a closer look.

"Yum!" said Kat, reaching for a cake.

"Wait—" warned Rosie, but her friend had already taken one.

FLASH! A bright white light filled the air and, for a moment, all Rosie could see were flashing stars.

Kat dropped the cupcake and fell backward. Rosie rubbed at her eyes and ran to help her friend. "Are you alright?" she asked anxiously.

"Yes," said Kat, dusting herself off. "It was a trap! When someone touches a cupcake, it sets off a camera."

Now that they were closer, it was easy to see the camera hidden in a nearby bush.

"I bet I know who put it there too," said Kat. "Desdemona! She was hoping to get a picture of a greedy yeti. I hope she's not too disappointed to get a photo of me instead."

Rosie moved the camera so it was pointing away from the cupcakes, and they continued up the mountain. As the path got steeper, the air became colder. A family of tiny ice mice scurried across their path, and Rosie stopped to admire

their warm blue sweaters. "I wish I had one," she shivered. Her breath came out in little frosty puffs when she spoke.

The animals that lived here were different from the ones in the forest below. Rosie spotted a bright blue ostrich sitting on a straggly nest. It was covered in fluffy feathers and Rosie caught a glimpse of three enormous eggs tucked under its warm body.

"Do you think it's a frostrich?" giggled Kat.

Puffing and panting, the girls' scrambled over a steep pile of rocks and finally reached the animal the crystalzoometers were leading them to ...

It was Snowball! The little yeti was sitting on a rock beside a plate of cupcakes. He looked very sorry for himself.

"He must have set off one of Desdemona's traps," said Kat. She tried to help the yeti stand, but he was too wobbly. "I think the flash hurt his eyes," she said.

"We'll take him to the vet's," Rosie said. "I think he might have bruised his arm too."

The girls took turns carrying Snowball down the mountain. It was strange to see him so quiet. At the bottom of the mountain, they stopped to get their bearings.

Rosie hadn't walked this way before, but she knew where to go. "We can cross the

Rainbow River on these stepping stones, then walk round the edge of Mazewood," she said. She had no plans to go into Mazewood— the trees and bushes were bewitched to keep changing places. Once inside, you might never find a way out!

Snowball perked up when they reached the stepping stones. Each stone rang out a musical note when it was stepped on, and the little yeti tried to sing along.

At last, the girls reached Flutterpuff Oak, the old tree that led to the surgery. Quibble, the hospital porter, was standing outside. He was a funny little man who looked a bit like a tree stump. His moss-tache quivered when he spoke. "Oh dear, dear, dear," he twittered, looking at Snowball. "A hurt yeti? You'd better take him to Doctor Hart." He pressed a lump in the oak tree, and the bark moved aside to show the

spiral staircase that led down to the surgery.

Kindly Doctor Hart was the head vet at Calico Comfrey's. She was very surprised by the friendly creature. "Yetis are usually so shy," she exclaimed. While she made a sling for Snowball's bruised arm, Rosie told her all about Desdemona and the camera traps.

Doctor Hart shook her head as she listened. "I can't think how someone like that got into the forest," she said at last. "I hope nothing's wrong with the forget-me-dos."

"Forget-me-dos?" asked Rosie.

"The blue flowers that grow around the edge of the forest," explained Doctor Hart. "My grandfather—Calico Comfrey—planted them long ago. It's their scent that makes people turn away at the edge of the forest."

Rosie gasped. "Her stinky necklace! It's so strong that she can't smell the flowers."

Chapter 7
Dad in the Forest

Snowball was soon feeling better. He started to explore the surgery, crawling under cushions and hiding in cupboards until Doctor Hart threw up her hands and said, "Enough! It's time this cheeky little yeti went home."

"His parents will be worried," said Kat.

"So will my dad," said Rosie feeling guilty.

"Snowball and I will walk you as far as Soft Henge," said Doctor Hart. "It's close to your campsite. We won't use the flying carpet, in case there are any more camera traps."

Soft Henge was the mysterious structure that the girls had first seen the night before.

Doctor Hart told them all about it as they passed by. "It is full of ancient magic," she said in hushed tones. "It was built many centuries ago by druids called the Whistling Warlocks. If you hum the right tune, it will instantly transport you to the other circles they made—Deep Henge, Bright Henge, or Cloud Henge."

"Is it safe?" asked Rosie.

"It is," smiled the vet. "But its magic is old and strange. Most of the animals in the forest won't go near it."

As the campsite
came into sight,
Rosie noticed
the blue forget-
me-dos growing
under the trees.
Snowball picked one
and tucked it behind his ear, looking very
pleased with himself.

"Why don't the forget-me-dos work on me
and Kat?" Rosie asked.

"Good question," said Doctor Hart. "That's
what we've been researching in the forest.
We *think* it's because you usually enter the
forest through the gate in your yard. You see,
Willow Cottage used to belong to my
grandfather, Calico Comfrey, so he didn't
plant any forget-me-dos there."

"Oh," said Rosie, feeling disappointed.

"I thought it was because Kat and I were special."

"You're definitely special," laughed the vet. "That gate is only visible to people who are true friends to animals. Anyone else just sees overgrown bushes."

"But we came in through the campsite today," said Kat.

"If you spend a lot of time in the forest, the scent of the forget-me-dos stops working on you," Doctor Hart replied. "It doesn't affect me—or the animals that live here."

Rosie suddenly had a wonderful idea. She explained it to Doctor Hart, who smiled and nodded. Then Rosie and Kat said goodbye and ran the rest of the way to the campsite.

"How would you like to see a yeti, Dad?" Rosie called. She fetched a clothespin, and popped it on his nose. Would her plan work?

To Rosie's delight, Dad walked right past the blue flowers and into the forest.

"What are they?" he asked in amazement, as three yellow flutterpuffs flittered overhead.

Rosie took the clothespin off his nose. "We've got so much to show you," she said.

They crossed the Rainbow River on the wooden footbridge and started to climb the winding mountain path. Kat pointed out the little ice mice in their adorable sweaters, scurrying here and there. Dad was astonished, excited, and confused—all at the same time. He rubbed his eyes as if he was dreaming, and murmured, "Goodness me," over and over again.

Suddenly, there were two loud trumpets from the path ahead.

"Watch out," Dad said suddenly. "That's a flummox." He pulled Rosie out of the way

as a large creature with shaggy, purple hair
thumped into sight. It stopped when it saw
them and gave two more trumpets. It looks
a bit like a woolly mammoth, Rosie thought.
Then, she noticed that it had a trunk and
tusks at each end!

"How do you know what a flummox is?"
Kat asked.

"Er … I'm not sure," Dad said scratching
his head.

As they climbed higher up the mountain, patches of snow started to appear on the ground. No wonder Snowball has such a thick, furry coat, Rosie thought, pulling on a sweater. She hoped that they would bump into him soon. She really liked the mischievous little creature.

A faint tinkling noise drifted toward them, and everyone stopped to listen. It seemed to be coming from a strange sort of treehouse with a platform that circled the trunk of an enormous oak. As she got closer, Rosie realized that the sound was coming from the silver windchimes that hung around it. The letters "C.C." were carved into the wood.

"Calico Comfrey!" Kat said. "He must have built this."

Excitedly, they all climbed the steps that spiralled up the trunk to the platform.

"What a view," Dad said, gazing across the mountainside. "Just look at those birds flying around the top of the mountain."

"Um ... Dad?" giggled Rosie. "I don't think they're birds."

Dad took out his binoculars for a closer look. "Goodness me," he said rubbing his eyes. "You're right, pumpkin. They're dragons!"

They took turns with the binoculars, watching the dragons until they vanished from sight among the crystal caves at the foot of the mountain.

Slowly, Dad clambered down the steps to the ground. He looked a bit dazed.

"Are you alright, Dad?" Rosie asked following him.

"Oh yes," he said. "It's just a lot to take in. All this time, I thought you two were making up stories about magical animals living in the forest. But they were all true."

"Yes," said Rosie. "And now you can meet them too."

"What a day," said Dad, giving Rosie a hug. "Whatever will your mother say?"

Kat started to climb down the spiral steps, and Rosie wondered if she was thinking about her parents. Did she want them to visit the forest too? Rosie knew they loved animals—after all, they had almost an entire zoo at home! But before she could ask, Dad gave a shout.

"I spy yetis!" he said waving his arms. "And one of them is wearing my cap!"

"Snowball!" shouted Rosie happily, rushing down to meet him. The little yeti had brought three friends with him. They seemed very shy and hid behind Dad's legs while Snowball investigated the contents of his backpack.

"No snacks, I'm afraid," Dad said. "But I've got the flying spinner. Do you like playing catch?"

It turned out that Snowball liked playing it very much!

Snowball hurled the flying spinner as hard as he could and it went whooshing straight up into the air, then landed on the roof of the treehouse.

"I'll get it," laughed Kat.

Rosie followed her up the steps to lend a hand, but stopped halfway. She could see a figure moving quickly along the mountain path. It was Desdemona—and she was holding one of her camera traps.

"Dad!" Rosie squeaked. "Look out!"

But it was too late—Desdemona had seen the yetis. There was a loud clatter, as the plate of cupcakes she was carrying fell to the floor. "I've found them," she shouted. "I was right all along. I'll be on the bestseller lists again!"

The baby yetis gave a little yelp and raced for the shelter of a nearby cave.

Only Snowball stayed where he was, looking curiously at the newcomer.

Dad stepped protectively in front of him and gave Desdemona a suspicious glance. "Dodo, isn't it?" he said. "From the campsite?"

"Deedee, my darling," chirruped Desdemona. "Now stand back. I have a very important photograph to take." She started to untangle the cables of her camera trap that were looped around her arm.

"Hide!" Rosie called from the platform.

Snowball didn't seem to understand what she was saying. He gave a happy growl and bounded up the steps toward her and Kat.

Desdemona looked on in astonishment. "Is this yeti your friend?" she asked. "How wonderful. Don't move a muscle. Let me untie these wires, then I'll get a shot of you all together." She started to yank at the tangle of cables again, and ...

POP! POP! POP! The camera's flash exploded in a burst of sound and light.

"Oh dear," muttered Desdemona. "I hope it's not broken."

But that was the least of her worries. There was an alarming rumble from somewhere higher up the mountain and, all at once, an avalanche of white snow came thundering down the path toward them!

"Help!" screamed Desdemona, racing up the steps of the treehouse to safety.

Rosie's Dad was about to follow her when he saw that one of the yetis had come out of the cave and was standing in the avalanche's path. Quick as a flash, he snatched it up and carried it back inside. Just in time! A moment later, the avalanche crashed down, blocking the cave's entrance with thick, heavy snow.

Chapter 8
A Toboggan Ride

Rosie stared down from the treehouse in shock. Only a moment ago, the ground had been covered with grass—now it was white with snow. Snowball began to whimper, and Kat picked him up and gave him a reassuring hug.

To her relief, Dad's muffled voice drifted out of the cave. "Are you okay, pumpkin?"

"I'm fine, Dad," she called back.

"How about you?"

"All good," said Dad. "The baby yetis are a bit scared, but nobody's hurt. Do you think you can dig us out?"

"We'll try," said Rosie.

The girls hurried down the treehouse steps and found that they were up to their knees in thick snow. They waded across to the cave's entrance, and Snowball scampered after them. He looked sad to hear his friends' whimpers coming from the cave.

Desdemona came down to help them dig. She was unusually quiet. "I'm sorry," she said eventually. "This is all my fault."

Kat glared at her. "Yes, it is," she said. "Those camera traps aren't safe."

The writer looked ashamed. "I feel terrible," she said. "I only wanted a picture for my book ..."

Rosie's fingers were starting to feel like blocks of ice. She wished she had a shovel— or a pair of gloves. "It's no good," she said, as her teeth began to chatter. "There's t-t-too much snow. We'll have to fetch the vets."

"The magical rescue vets from your stories?" came Dad's muffled voice from the cave. "They're real too?"

"Of course they are," said Kat. "Don't worry. They'll know what to do."

But the path down the mountain that they had climbed so easily was now covered in deep, slippery snow. It would be a dangerous descent.

"If only we had your brothers' toboggan," Rosie sighed.

Kat thought for a moment. "We don't need it," she said, her eyes lighting up. "It looks like the avalanche has broken off a chunk of the treehouse. We can use that."

Rosie gulped. It was a long way down the mountain. But Kat was already pulling the wood out of the snow and checking to see if it would take their weight. Snowball thought this was a great game.

"Don't worry," said Desdemona. "I'll stay here to keep your dad safe."

"Thank you," said Rosie, carefully climbing on behind Kat—and Snowball.

Kat pushed off with her feet, and the toboggan began to zoom down the mountainside.

"Wheeeee!" squeaked Snowball. He was having the time of his life!

The wind whipped through Rosie's hair as they whooshed along on the top of the snow. Faster and faster, they sped down the path, and Rosie was just beginning to think she might be enjoying herself … when she saw that the snow beneath them was starting to run out.

"How do we stop this thing?" she yelled.

"I don't know," her friend called back. "Hold on tight."

Rosie clung on, trying not to panic. She was sure the toboggan would throw them off when they reached the grass. After all, you couldn't toboggan over a meadow ... Could you?

The green grass of Moonflower Meadow got closer and closer, but the toboggan showed no sign of stopping. It sped smoothly over the lush, spring grass and flowers, and headed for the Rainbow River. Rosie gulped and braced herself for a splash— but it didn't come. To her astonishment, the toboggan just flew over the river and sped on into the forest.

"This wood must be enchanted," she shouted.

Now the toboggan was zigzagging this way and that, dodging between the trees. It was like riding on a very peculiar roller coaster.

"Help!" Rosie shouted. "We're heading into Mazewood."

But there was nothing they could do. The toboggan sped on, as if it was being pulled by a magnet. The dark trees flashed past, and Rosie caught sight of a pair of red eyes

peering out at her from the branches. Then, as if by magic, a large bush appeared in front of them blocking the way.

"We're going to crash!" wailed Kat.

With a jolt, the toboggan swerved to the right, missing the bush but sending itself into a spin. It gave a little shake, then gathered speed again, shooting out of Mazewood and screeching to a halt at the foot of Flutterpuff Oak. Snowball and the girls tumbled off the wood and lay on the ground, laughing and breathless from their amazing ride.

"Oh my spoons and jars!" came a voice. "What an extraordinary entrance." Rosie looked up and was pleased to see Doctor Morel's familiar face, with his large glasses and pointy hat. The gnome vet peered at Rosie through his large glasses. "Are you alright?" he asked.

Scrambling to her feet, Rosie started to explain about the avalanche, but she was interrupted by the swoosh of the flying carpet. It glided toward her in a stream of rainbow bubbles with Doctor Clarice at the front.

"Our crystalzoometers have been going wild," said Doctor Clarice. "Do you girls have any ideas what is going on?"

Rosie started to explain all over again.

"Oh my pots and pans," said Doctor Morel, throwing up his hands in horror. "We'll need blankets, shovels, and hot water bottles. Wait here!"

While he fetched the equipment, Kat showed Doctor Clarice the wood that had taken them down the mountain and explained what had happened. The vet studied it carefully.

"Calico Comfrey must have built that treehouse out of homewood," she said. "It's a magical wood that has the ability to return home if it is broken or damaged."

Snowball loved the rainbow bubbles that popped and spluttered from the back of the carpet. He reached up to pop them with his paws, and he giggled when they burst on his nose.

The girls helped Doctor Morel load up the flying carpet, then scrambled on board.

Kat looked at the shovels. "I don't suppose these are … magic shovels?" she asked.

Doctor Clarice shook her head. "Are you worried about how much snow there is to clear?" she asked. "There's something in my workshop that might help. Do you remember the de-messifier?"

Rosie and Kat nodded. It had helped them clear up all the bubbles from washing the bugbears in no time. "Would it work on snow?" asked Rosie curiously.

"It's worth a try," said Doctor Clarice.

Doctor Morel disappeared back into the surgery one last time and came back with the shiny de-messifier. Then, with a wobble, the flying carpet moved into the air and rose above the trees.

As they neared the mountains, Doctor Morel asked which one the cave was on.

"The one closest to the Rainbow River," said Rosie.

"That'll be Old Snowtumble," said Doctor Morel. "I might have guessed!"

"Do all the Cotton-Top Mountains have different names?" asked Kat curiously.

"Of course they do!" said Doctor Morel. "Look, that one's Tangleweather, and beside it is Short Rock, and Gembottom. Of course, those are just the gnome names," he added. "The dragons have completely different names for them all."

It was hard to know where to land on the blanket of white snow until they saw Desdemona. She waved her arms when she spotted them, and she guided them down to a safe landing on the soft snow by the treehouse.

"A flying carpet!" she said, her eyes lighting up. She stared at Doctor Morel, who was clambering down from the carpet. "Are you ... a genie?"

"I most certainly am not," said the little gnome huffily.

"Neither am I," added Doctor Clarice quickly.

Luckily, Dad's voice interrupted them. "Rosie? Kat?" he called. "That was fast!"

"How are the yetis?" called Rosie.

"Cuddled up on my lap to keep warm," said Dad. "Can you get us out of here?"

Doctor Clarice held up the de-messifier, just like she had done in the surgery. It began to spin, glinting and shining in the sunlight, and as it did, the snow started to whirr around like a mini blizzard. As it whooshed, it clumped together, forming an enormous snowball—which Snowball immediately sat on! In no time at all, the entrance was clear. Rosie rushed over to give her dad a hug.

Chapter 9
Snowball's Pillow

Feeling very grown up, Rosie introduced Dad to Doctor Morel and Doctor Clarice. They all shook hands politely. Then she introduced Desdemona Downspout.

"Rainbows and roses, I've heard of you," said Doctor Morel. "You wrote a book about the Loch Ness Monster."

"Have you read it?" asked Desdemona.

"Yes," said Doctor Morel sternly. "And I've never read such nonsense in my life. I'll have you know that Nessie is a good friend of mine and would never do half the things you say in the book."

Desdemona looked astonished. She was about to say something else when Doctor Clarice looked down at her crystalzoometer. "There's more work to do, I'm afraid," she said. "It seems the avalanche has caused problems for other creatures further down the mountain."

"I'm so sorry about all this," said Desdemona. She looked very guilty. "How can I help?"

Doctor Clarice handed her a flask of hot milk and some mugs. "Help Kat and Rosie look after the yetis," she said. "Doctor Morel and I will be back soon."

It wasn't long before the flying carpet was back, carrying Doctor Clarice and a family of shivering ice mice.

"I'm taking them back to the surgery for observation," she said. "They were buried in a big heap of snow."

"Where's Doctor Morel?" Kat asked.

"I dropped him off at Gnome Town," said Doctor Clarice. "A family of flummoxes were scared by the avalanche and they're causing chaos down there. He'll sort things out! Are we ready to go?"

Rosie said goodbye to the baby yetis. Now that they were feeling better, they were eager to get away. They were too shy to be comfortable around so many people! One gave her a tiny hug, then they all scampered off into the shadows. Only Snowball stayed behind, snuffling happily around everyone's

feet. He really was a most unusual yeti!

Snowball watched Rosie fetch another blanket for the ice mice. He darted away into the cave and came back with something that looked like a small, white pillow. He placed it gently on the flying carpet.

"Awww," said Kat. "He wants to help."

But Doctor Clarice was shocked. "Oh, Snowball!" she said. "Is that a Portal Pillow?"

Snowball looked very embarrassed. He blushed and stared down at his feet.

"From the look on his face, I'd say that it is," said Dad. "But, er, what is a Portal Pillow?"

"It's one of the pillows from Soft Henge," Doctor Clarice replied. She explained that they could be used to move instantly from one place in the forest to another. "But it's a terrible way to travel," she added. "You never know where you'll go. It could be at the top of a tree, or in the Rainbow River—

or deep in the heart of Mazewood. Most creatures wouldn't dare take one."

"Snowball loves adventures," said Rosi giving him a hug. "I think he's been using the Portal Pillows to explore." She remembered how he had vanished so mysteriously when they were at Soft Henge. That must have been when he picked this one up.

"So all the yeti sightings Desdemona told us about were probably ... just him," said Kat slowly.

Rosie nodded. It seemed more likely than Desdemona's idea that the forest was "crammed" with yetis. She wondered how Desdemona would react. Would she be upset—or angry? To her relief, the writer roared with laughter. She was as unpredictable as a Portal Pillow, Rosie thought!

It was very crowded with so many people on the flying carpet. Doctor Clarice sat at the front, and Dad, Desdemona, Snowball, Kat, and Rosie squeezed in behind her, holding the ice mice on their laps.

"This will be a wonderful chapter in my book," murmured Desdemona happily, as they soared into the sky. Rosie and Kat exchanged worried looks.

"About that ..." said Doctor Clarice firmly. "I need to tell you about the last time word got out about Starfall Forest."

"Well, I do like stories," said Desdemona.

"A long time ago, magical creatures lived in enchanted forests all over the world," said Doctor Clarice. "But greedy people wanted the magic for themselves. Countless trees were cut down, and many animals were caught in traps and taken from their homes!

Calico Comfrey brought
the remaining creatures
to live in Starfall Forest,
and for a while, all was well. Then—twenty-
five years ago—a newspaper published an
article about his work. Before long, people
from all over the world arrived in the forest
looking for the magical animals. And it began
again—cutting down trees, stealing animals.
That was when Calico Comfrey planted the
forget-me-dos at the edge of the forest—to
keep people out for good."

"How awful," said Rosie. She remembered the newspaper clippings she had seen in Desdemona's motor home and realized that they must have been from that terrible time.

"It happened long before I came to work at the surgery," said Doctor Clarice sadly. "Doctor Morel and Doctor Hart told me all about it. That's why we try so hard to keep the secret of Starfall Forest safe."

Rosie heard a sob and turned to see Desdemona wiping tears from her eyes.

"Oh dear," she sniffed. "That was a very sad story. Do you think that … perhaps … I shouldn't write my book?"

"Of course you shouldn't," groaned Kat. "If you do, people will trample all over the forest again and it will be your fault."

"But what about my career?" wailed Desdemona.

"Now, now," said Rosie's Dad, patting the writer on the shoulder in a kindly way. "You can still write a book about yetis. Just don't say that it's true."

"Dad, you're a genius!" said Rosie. "I bet Desdemona's publisher would love a children's book about Snowball."

Desdemona stopped crying immediately. She pulled out a large, purple handkerchief and blew her nose. "I can picture the cover already," she said. "I'll call it The Most Unusual Yeti."

Desdemona promised not to reveal the secret of the forest in her book and she gave Snowball a little pat on his head. "I couldn't bear it if any animals were hurt because of me," she said.

With a whoosh of air, the flying carpet swooped down and landed beside the mysterious shapes of Soft Henge. Snowball's pillow started to glow ...

"It's glad to be back home," Doctor Clarice said. "It probably needs to recharge its magic."

A soft hum filled the air, and Soft Henge began to glow too. A cloud of flutterbys that had settled on one of the pillows flew up into the air, making beautiful shapes as they flitted away through the trees.

Desdemona stared around her in wonder. "It's beautiful," she said.

"Yes," said Dad. "I'm not a huge fan of

portal travel, though. It makes me feel sick."

"Dad!" said Rosie. "When have you ever been in a portal?"

"Sorry, pumpkin," Dad shook his head. "I don't know why I said that."

Snowball snuffled around edge of the circle, searching for the right place to put the pillow. As soon as it was back in position, the humming stopped, and Soft Henge's mystical glow started to fade ...

Doctor Clarice waved goodbye and flew back to the surgery with Snowball and the ice mice. The others walked slowly back to the campsite. Desdemona made a note of Dad's address and promised to send a copy of her book as soon as it was published. "I know that it is going to be a bestseller!" she said.

Rosie and Kat helped Dad take down the tarpaulin and pack everything into the car. It was very quiet without Snowball—but they probably got everything done much faster than they would have if he was snuffling around their feet.

Kat didn't say much on the drive back home and Rosie wondered if anything was wrong. They stopped outside Kat's house, and Dad helped carry her bags to the front door. Buttons came out to greet her, twining

himself around her legs, while Bertie sat on the windowsill licking his paws.

"What's the matter?" Rosie eventually asked. "Are you sad that the trip's over?"

Kat gave a big sigh. "I was thinking ..." she said. "It's great that your dad came with us today. I just wish my dad had been there too. And Mama! She would have loved to meet Snowball."

Chapter 10
An Amazing Picnic

The next day was Sunday, and Rosie's mother was home from Opal City bright and early. Rosie rushed to give her a huge hug.

"Welcome home," Dad called. "You're just in time for breakfast. I'm making pancakes!"

"That sounds wonderful," said Mama putting down her bags. "I can't wait to hear all about your trip." She didn't seem to notice the purple groak that was hopping up the path behind her. Rosie grinned. Sometimes the groaks kept her awake at night with their tuba-like honking, but they were so cute, she didn't really mind. The groak dropped a little white card on the doormat, and hopped quickly away.

"What's this?" Mama said, picking up the card. "We're all invited to a Doctor Hart's tea party in the forest—this afternoon."

"That's one of the vets I'm always telling you about," said Rosie. "Can we go? Please?"

They were interrupted by the sound of the telephone. Dad answered it. "It's Kat," he called. "Her family has been invited too!"

Kat was fizzing with excitement when she arrived at Willow Cottage later that day with her parents. Brianna and the twins were staying with her grandparents.

Rosie led everyone through the overgrown yard, ducking under low branches and pushing past spiky bushes until they reached the path that led to the toad gate.

"We're nearly at the gate to the forest," Rosie announced. A worrying thought had entered her mind. If true friends to animals could see the gate, why hadn't her parents seen it before now?

"Do you mean that old gate with the toad on it?" asked Dad.

Rosie felt relief wash over her. Of course her dad was a true friend to animals! How silly of her to think anything else. "Yes, that's it," she said. "Er ... can you see it too, Mama?"

"Of course I can," smiled her mother. "I noticed it the first day we moved in."

"But you've never tried to go through it?" Rosie asked in astonishment.

Her mother blushed. "We've been very busy," she said.

Kat's parents saw the gate too, and Rosie gripped her friend's hand tightly as they walked into the forest all together for the first time.

As soon as they entered the forest, there was a fluttering noise in the trees overhead. A crowd of little fluffballs came tumbling toward them on tiny wings, each one a different shade of the rainbow. Kat's parents stared in amazement at the odd-looking creatures that twittered around their heads.

"These are flutterpuffs," said Rosie. "I think they've come to take us to the tea party!"

The little creatures led them through the trees to Flutterpuff Oak, where Doctor Morel and Doctor Clarice were waiting with a picnic blanket. There were pretty plates of sandwiches, overflowing bowls of fruit, and piles of crumbly cookies.

"Hello, hello," said Doctor Morel. "Oh my stars and slippers, isn't it a nice day for a tea party?"

Kat's mother jumped as Quibble appeared

from a hole in the side of the tree carrying
a large pot of tea.

"He's the surgery's porter," hissed Kat.

"P-pleased to meet you, Mr. Tree-Stump,"
stammered her mother.

"I'm sure you have lots of questions," said
Doctor Clarice kindly. "We will answer them
all, but first, please do sit down and have
some food."

"If anyone needs to sit down, it's me," Doctor Morel muttered. "I had to walk all the way home from Gnome Town yesterday after I helped those flustered flummoxes."

Rosie and Kat sat down and started to load their plates with delicious looking treats, while Quibble poured them each a glass of lemonade.

Doctor Hart appeared holding a tray full of toad-shaped cookies. "Welcome, everyone," she said, her kindly face crinkling into a smile. Then, she saw Rosie's dad and her smile widened. "Why, hello Jeremy," she said. "I haven't seen you for a long time."

Rosie looked at her dad in surprise. "You know each other?" she asked.

"Of course," said Doctor Hart. "Young Jeremy here used to help out in the surgery all the time when he was a boy."

Rosie's Dad looked very puzzled. He rubbed his eyes, and blinked. "I ... I'd forgotten," he said slowly. "It's all coming back to me. Yes, yes, of course. I used to visit every weekend to help you and your grandfather. Then, my family moved to Opal City ..." He paused, shaking his head. "How could I have forgotten all this?"

Rosie's mother smiled. "You didn't forget completely," she said. "You've always talked about how magical Springhaven is. That's why you wanted us to move here."

"In the forest yesterday, I had the strangest feeling that I'd been there before," Dad admitted. "Now, everything's starting to come back to me." He screwed up his face as if he was thinking really hard. "There was that trouble with the Snow Bear that wouldn't hibernate ... And the time I got lost in Mazewood ... But the last thing I remember was planting all those flowers with Doctor Comfrey."

"Of course," said Doctor Hart. "You helped Grandfather plant the forget-me-dos. It was the day before your family moved to Opal City. The smell must have affected your memory."

Rosie could hardly believe it. Her dad had worked with the vets! He had been lost in Mazewood! He had even known the mysterious Calico Comfrey ... She threw her arms around him and gave him a huge hug.

"Like father, like daughter, eh, pumpkin?" he said.

Doctor Hart smiled. "You should be very proud of her," she said. "She and Kat work so hard to care for the forest's animals."

"Will we be able to meet the little yeti we've heard so much about?" said Kat's mother.

"Of course," said Doctor Clarice. "I'll fetch the flying carpet." Rosie noticed that her eyes were shining in the way they always did when she had a new invention to try out.

When she returned, there was a comfy-looking beanbag attached to the carpet.

"I call this the Pipsqueak," Doctor Clarice said proudly. "Anyone who sits on it will shrink down to the size of a mouse until they get off again. It means that we can fit lots of people on the carpet with no trouble. I had to invent something," she added with a grin. "It was really crowded yesterday with the ice mice on our laps!"

Rosie's Dad was the first to try out the Pipsqueak. Gingerly, he lowered himself down and waited. Flash! Bang! A cloud

of red smoke puffed out of the beanbag
and hid him from view. When it cleared,
normal-sized Dad was gone and in his place
was a mouse-sized version.

"Anyone got any cheese?" squeaked Dad
in a tiny voice, showing his front teeth and
making a nibbling noise.

Rosie sat on the beanbag next, and the others followed. It was very strange to be the size of a mouse. The trees suddenly seemed like skyscrapers, and Doctor Clarice was a giant with a loud, booming voice.

"Next stop, Old Snowtumble," rumbled the vet. "I'll land beside Calico Comfrey's old treehouse. I think Snowball and his family live nearby. Most of the snow will have melted by now."

"Already?" asked Kat's dad in surprise.

"There's magic in the mountain air," said Doctor Clarice with a smile. "I wouldn't be surprised if the snow was enchanted too."

The vet was right. She landed the carpet on grass and flowers, and the only snow to be seen on any of the Cotton-Top Mountains was at the very top.

Rosie took hold of Kat's hand and together,

they slid down the beanbag onto the carpet with a swoosh! As soon as their feet touched the floor, there was another puff of smoke and they were back to their usual size.

There was a friendly roar from the rocks above, and Snowball came bounding down to greet them. He flung himself into Rosie's arms and nuzzled into her neck.

"Look!" Kat's mother whispered suddenly.

Two large yetis were standing in the shadows by the treehouse. One gave a shy wave, then they both disappeared from view.

"That must be Snowball's parents," said Doctor Clarice. "What a privilege. Very few people have ever seen an adult yeti."

The amazed looks on everyone's faces made Rosie laugh! She took Kat's hand and gave it a happy squeeze. She was so pleased that their parents finally knew the secret of Starfall Forest—and that the vets trusted them all to keep it safe. She couldn't wait for their next adventure.